'I said that although hanging Colby was almost certainly against the law, we had a perfect *moral* right to do so because he was *our* friend, *belonged* to us in various important senses, and he had after all gone too far'

DONALD BARTHELME
Born 7 April 1931, Philadelphia, USA
Died 23 July 1989, Houston, USA

'Chablis' first appeared in *The New Yorker*. 'Margins' first
appeared in *Come Back, Dr. Caligari*. 'The Balloon' and
'Game' first appeared in *Unspeakable Practices, Unnatural Acts*.
'The Glass Mountain' first appeared in *City Life* and 'I Bought
a Little City' and 'The School' first appeared in *Amateurs*.

ALSO PUBLISHED BY PENGUIN BOOKS
Forty Stories · Sixty Stories

DONALD BARTHELME

Some of Us Had Been Threatening Our Friend Colby

PENGUIN BOOKS

PENGUIN CLASSICS

Published by the Penguin Group
Penguin Books Ltd, 80 Strand, London WC2R 0RL, England
Penguin Group (USA), Inc., 375 Hudson Street, New York, New York 10014, USA
Penguin Group (Canada), 90 Eglinton Avenue East, Suite 700, Toronto, Ontario,
Canada M4P 2Y3 (a division of Pearson Penguin Canada Inc.)
Penguin Ireland, 25 St Stephen's Green, Dublin 2, Ireland (a division of Penguin Books Ltd)
Penguin Group (Australia), 250 Camberwell Road, Camberwell, Victoria 3124, Australia
(a division of Pearson Australia Group Pty Ltd)
Penguin Books India Pvt Ltd, 11 Community Centre, Panchsheel Park,
New Delhi – 110 017, India
Penguin Group (NZ), 67 Apollo Drive, Rosedale, North Shore 0632, New Zealand
(a division of Pearson New Zealand Ltd)
Penguin Books (South Africa) (Pty) Ltd, 24 Sturdee Avenue, Rosebank, Johannesburg 2196,
South Africa

Penguin Books Ltd, Registered Offices: 80 Strand, London WC2R 0RL, England

www.penguin.com

'The Palace at 4 A.M.', 'Chablis' and 'Some of Us Had Been Threatening Our
Friend Colby' selected from Sixty Stories, published in Penguin Classics 2003
'The Glass Mountain', 'I Bought a Little City', 'The School', 'Margins', 'Game' and
'The Balloon' selected from Forty Stories, published in Penguin Classics 2005
This edition published in Penguin Classics 2011

3

The author's estate is grateful to Little, Brown and Company for permission to reprint
the story 'Margins' from Come Back, Dr. Caligari and to Farrar, Straus & Giroux, Inc. for
permission to reprint the stories 'The Balloon' and 'Game' from Unspeakable Practices,
Unnatural Acts; 'The Glass Mountain' from City Life; and 'I Bought a Little City' and
'The School' from Amateurs.

Copyright © Donald Barthelme, 1981, 1982, 1987

Typeset by Jouve (UK), Milton Keynes
Printed in England by Clays Ltd, St Ives plc

ISBN: 978-0-141-19577-3

www.greenpenguin.co.uk

Penguin Books is committed to a sustainable future
for our business, our readers and our planet.
The book in your hands is made from paper
certified by the Forest Stewardship Council.

Contents

*Some of Us Had Been Threatening
Our Friend Colby* I

The Glass Mountain 9

I Bought a Little City 17

The Palace at Four A.M. 27

Chablis 39

The School 45

Margins 51

Game 59

The Balloon 67

Some of Us Had Been Threatening Our Friend Colby

Some of us had been threatening our friend Colby for a long time, because of the way he had been behaving. And now he'd gone too far, so we decided to hang him. Colby argued that just because he had gone too far (he did not deny that he had gone too far) did not mean that he should be subjected to hanging. Going too far, he said, was something everybody did sometimes. We didn't pay much attention to this argument. We asked him what sort of music he would like played at the hanging. He said he'd think about it but it would take him a while to decide. I pointed out that we'd have to know soon, because Howard, who is a conductor, would have to hire and rehearse the musicians and he couldn't begin until he knew what the music was going to be. Colby said he'd always been fond of Ives's Fourth Symphony. Howard said that this was a 'delaying tactic' and that everybody knew that the Ives was almost impossible to perform and would involve weeks of rehearsal, and that the size of the orchestra and chorus would put us way over the music budget. 'Be reasonable,' he said to Colby. Colby said he'd try to think of something a little less exacting.

Hugh was worried about the wording of the invitations. What if one of them fell into the hands of the authorities? Hanging Colby was doubtless against the law, and if the authorities learned in advance what the plan was they would very likely come in and try to mess everything up. I said that although hanging Colby was almost certainly against the law, we had a perfect *moral* right to do so because he was *our* friend, *belonged* to us in various important senses, and he had after all gone too far. We agreed that the invitations would be worded in such a way that the person invited could not know for sure what he was being invited to. We decided to refer to the event as 'An Event Involving Mr Colby Williams.' A handsome script was selected from a catalogue and we picked a cream-colored paper. Magnus said he'd see to having the invitations printed, and wondered whether we should serve drinks. Colby said he thought drinks would be nice but was worried about the expense. We told him kindly that the expense didn't matter, that we were after all his dear friends and if a group of his dear friends couldn't get together and do the thing with a little bit of *éclat*, why, what was the world coming to? Colby asked if he would be able to have drinks, too, before the event. We said, 'Certainly.'

The next item of business was the gibbet. None of us knew too much about gibbet design, but Tomás, who is an architect, said he'd look it up in old books and draw the plans. The important thing, as far as he recollected, was that the trapdoor function perfectly. He said that just roughly, counting labor and materials, it shouldn't run us more than four hundred dollars. 'Good God!' Howard said. He said what was Tomás figuring on, rosewood? No, just a good grade of pine, Tomás said. Victor asked if unpainted pine wouldn't look kind of 'raw,' and Tomás replied that he thought it could be stained a dark walnut without too much trouble.

I said that although I thought the whole thing ought to be done really well and all, I also thought four hundred dollars for a gibbet, on top of the expense for the drinks, invitations, musicians, and everything, was a bit steep, and why didn't we just use a tree – a nice-looking oak, or something? I pointed out that since it was going to be a June hanging the trees would be in glorious leaf and that not only would a tree add a kind of 'natural' feeling but it was also strictly traditional, especially in the West. Tomás, who had been sketching gibbets on

3

the backs of envelopes, reminded us that an outdoor hanging always had to contend with the threat of rain. Victor said he liked the idea of doing it outdoors, possibly on the bank of a river, but noted that we would have to hold it some distance from the city, which presented the problem of getting the guests, musicians, etc., to the site and then back to town.

At this point everybody looked at Harry, who runs a car-and-truck-rental business. Harry said he thought he could round up enough limousines to take care of that end but that the drivers would have to be paid. The drivers, he pointed out, wouldn't be friends of Colby's and couldn't be expected to donate their services, any more than the bartender or the musicians. He said that he had about ten limousines, which he used mostly for funerals, and that he could probably obtain another dozen by calling around to friends of his in the trade. He said also that if we did it outside, in the open air, we'd better figure on a tent or awning of some kind to cover at least the principals and the orchestra, because if the hanging was being rained on he thought it would look kind of dismal. As between gibbet and tree, he said, he had no particular preferences and he really thought that the choice ought to be left up to Colby, since it was his hanging. Colby said that everybody went too far, sometimes, and weren't we being a little Draconian? Howard said rather sharply that all that had already been discussed, and which did he want, gibbet or tree? Colby asked if he could have a firing squad. No, Howard said, he could not. Howard said a firing squad would just be an ego trip for Colby, the blindfold and last-cigarette bit, and that Colby was in enough hot water already without trying to 'upstage' everyone with unnecessary theatrics. Colby said he was sorry, he hadn't meant it that way, he'd take the tree. Tomás crumpled up the gibbet sketches he'd been making, in disgust.

Then the question of the hangman came up. Pete said did we really need a hangman? Because if we used a tree, the noose could be adjusted to the appropriate level and Colby could just jump off something – a chair or stool or something. Besides, Pete said, he very much doubted if there were any free-lance hangmen wandering around the country, now that capital punishment has been done away with absolutely, temporarily, and that we'd probably have to fly one in from England or Spain or one of the South American countries, and even if we did that how could we know in advance that the man was a professional, a real hangman, and not just some money-hungry amateur who might bungle the job and shame us all, in front of everybody? We all agreed then that Colby should just jump off something and that a chair was not what he should jump off of, because that would look, we felt, extremely tacky – some old kitchen chair sitting out there under our beautiful tree. Tomás, who is quite modern in outlook and not afraid of innovation, proposed that Colby be standing on a large round rubber ball ten feet in diameter. This, he said, would afford a sufficient 'drop' and would also roll out of the way if Colby suddenly changed his mind after jumping off. He reminded us that by not using a regular hangman we were placing an awful lot of the responsibility for the success of the affair on Colby himself, and that although he was sure Colby would perform creditably and not disgrace his friends at the last minute, still, men have been known to get a little irresolute at times like that, and the ten-foot-round rubber ball, which could probably be fabricated rather cheaply, would insure a 'bang-up' production right down to the wire.

At the mention of 'wire,' Hank, who had been silent all this time, suddenly spoke up and said he wondered if it wouldn't be better if we used wire instead of rope – more efficient and in the end kinder to Colby, he suggested. Colby began looking a little green, and I didn't blame him, because there is something extremely distasteful in thinking about being hanged with wire instead of rope – it gives you a sort of a revulsion, when you think about it. I thought it was really quite unpleasant of Hank to be sitting there talking about wire, just when we had solved the problem of what Colby was going to jump off of so neatly, with Tomás's idea about the rubber ball, so I hastily said that wire was out of the question, because it would injure the tree – cut into the branch it was tied to when Colby's full weight hit it – and that in these days of increased respect for the environment, we didn't want that, did we? Colby gave me a grateful look, and the meeting broke up.

Everything went off very smoothly on the day of the event (the music Colby finally picked was standard stuff, Elgar, and it was played very well by Howard and his boys). It didn't rain, the event was well attended, and we didn't run out of Scotch, or anything. The ten-foot rubber ball had been painted a deep green and blended in well with the bucolic setting. The two things I remember best about the whole episode are the grateful look Colby gave me when I said what I said about the wire, and the fact that nobody has ever gone too far again.

The Glass Mountain

1. I was trying to climb the glass mountain.
2. The glass mountain stands at the corner of Thirteenth Street and Eighth Avenue.
3. I had attained the lower slope.
4. People were looking up at me.
5. I was new in the neighborhood.
6. Nevertheless I had acquaintances.
7. I had strapped climbing irons to my feet and each hand grasped a sturdy plumber's friend.
8. I was 200 feet up.
9. The wind was bitter.
10. My acquaintances had gathered at the bottom of the mountain to offer encouragement.
11. 'Shithead.'
12. 'Asshole.'
13. Everyone in the city knows about the glass mountain.
14. People who live here tell stories about it.
15. It is pointed out to visitors.

16. Touching the side of the mountain, one feels coolness.

17. Peering into the mountain, one sees sparkling blue-white depths.

18. The mountain towers over the part of Eighth Avenue like some splendid, immense office building.

19. The top of the mountain vanishes into the clouds, or on cloudless days, into the sun.

20. I unstuck the righthand plumber's friend leaving the left-hand one in place.

21. Then I stretched out and reattached the righthand one a little higher up, after which I inched my legs into new positions.

22. The gain was minimal, not an arm's length.

23. My acquaintances continued to comment.

24. 'Dumb motherfucker.'

25. I was new in the neighborhood.

26. In the streets were many people with disturbed eyes.

27. Look for yourself.

28. In the streets were hundreds of young people shooting up in doorways, behind parked cars.

29. Older people walked dogs.

30. The sidewalks were full of dogshit in brilliant colors: ocher, umber, Mars yellow, sienna, viridian, ivory black, rose madder.

31. And someone had been apprehended cutting down trees, a row of elms broken-backed among the VWs and Valiants.

32. Done with a power saw, beyond a doubt.

33. I was new in the neighborhood yet I had accumulated acquaintances.

34. My acquaintances passed a brown bottle from hand to hand.

35. 'Better than a kick in the crotch.'

36. 'Better than a poke in the eye with a sharp stick.'

37. 'Better than a slap in the belly with a wet fish.'

38. 'Better than a thump on the back with a stone.'

39. 'Won't he make a splash when he falls, now?'

40. 'I hope to be here to see it. Dip my handkerchief in the blood.'

41. 'Fart-faced fool.'

42. I unstuck the lefthand plumber's friend leaving the righthand one in place.

43. And reached out.

44. To climb the glass mountain, one first requires a good reason.

45. No one has ever climbed the mountain on behalf of science, or in search of celebrity, or because the mountain was a challenge.

46. Those are not good reasons.

47. But good reasons exist.

48. At the top of the mountain there is a castle of pure gold, and in a room in the castle tower sits . . .

49. My acquaintances were shouting at me.

50. 'Ten bucks you bust your ass in the next four minutes!'

51. . . . a beautiful enchanted symbol.

52. I unstuck the righthand plumber's friend leaving the lefthand one in place.

53. And reached out.

54. It was cold there at 206 feet and when I looked down I was not encouraged.

55. A heap of corpses both of horses and riders ringed the bottom of the mountain, many dying men groaning there.

56. 'A weakening of the libidinous interest in reality has recently come to a close.' (Anton Ehrenzweig)

57. A few questions burned in my mind.

58. Does one climb a glass mountain, at considerable personal discomfort, simply to disenchant a symbol?

59. Do today's stronger egos still *need* symbols?

60. I decided that the answer to these questions was 'yes.'

61. Otherwise what was I doing there, 206 feet above the power-sawed elms, whose white meat I could see from my height?

62. The best way to fail to climb the mountain is to be a knight in full armor – one whose horse's hoofs strike fiery sparks from the sides of the mountain.

63. The following-named knights had failed to climb the mountain and were groaning in the heap: Sir Giles Guilford, Sir Henry Lovell, Sir Albert Denny, Sir Nicholas Vaux, Sir Patrick Grifford, Sir Gisbourne Gower, Sir Thomas Grey, Sir Peter Coleville, Sir John Blunt, Sir Richard Vernon, Sir Walter Willoughby, Sir Stephen Spear, Sir Roger Faulconbridge, Sir Clarence Vaughan, Sir Hubert Ratcliffe, Sir James Tyrrel, Sir Walter Herbert, Sir Robert Brakenbury, Sir Lionel Beaufort, and many others.

64. My acquaintances moved among the fallen knights.

65. My acquaintances moved among the fallen knights, collecting rings, wallets, pocket watches, ladies' favors.

66. 'Calm reigns in the country, thanks to the confident wisdom of everyone.' (M. Pompidou)

67. The golden castle is guarded by a lean-headed eagle with blazing rubies for eyes.

68. I unstuck the lefthand plumber's friend, wondering if –

69. My acquaintances were prising out the gold teeth of not-yet-dead knights.

70. In the streets were people concealing their calm behind a façade of vague dread.

71. 'The conventional symbol (such as the nightingale, often associated with melancholy), even though it is recognized only through agreement, is not a sign

(like the traffic light) because, again, it presumably arouses deep feelings and is regarded as possessing properties beyond what the eye alone sees.' (*A Dictionary of Literary Terms*)

72. A number of nightingales with traffic lights tied to their legs flew past me.

73. A knight in pale-pink armor appeared above me.

74. He sank, his armor making tiny shrieking sounds against the glass.

75. He gave me a sideways glance as he passed me.

76. He uttered the word '*Muerte*' as he passed me.

77. I unstuck the righthand plumber's friend.

78. My acquaintances were debating the question, which of them would get my apartment?

79. I reviewed the conventional means of attaining the castle.

80. The conventional means of attaining the castle are as follows: 'The eagle dug its sharp claws into the tender flesh of the youth, but he bore the pain without a sound, and seized the bird's two feet with his hands. The creature in terror lifted him high up into the air and began to circle the castle. The youth held on bravely. He saw the glittering palace, which by the pale rays of the moon looked like a dim lamp; and he saw the windows and balconies of the castle tower. Drawing a small knife from his belt, he cut

off both the eagle's feet. The bird rose up in the air with a yelp, and the youth dropped lightly onto a broad balcony. At the same moment a door opened, and he saw a courtyard filled with flowers and trees, and there, the beautiful enchanted princess.' (*The Yellow Fairy Book*)

81. I was afraid.

82. I had forgotten the Band-Aids.

83. When the eagle dug its sharp claws into my tender flesh –

84. Should I go back for the Band-Aids?

85. But if I went back for the Band-Aids I would have to endure the contempt of my acquaintances.

86. I resolved to proceed without the Band-Aids.

87. 'In some centuries, his [man's] imagination has made life an intense practice of all the lovelier energies.' (John Masefield)

88. The eagle dug its sharp claws into my tender flesh.

89. But I bore the pain without a sound, and seized the bird's two feet with my hands.

90. The plumber's friends remained in place, standing at right angles to the side of the mountain.

91. The creature in terror lifted me high in the air and began to circle the castle.

92. I held on bravely.

93. I saw the glittering palace, which by the pale rays of

the moon looked like a dim lamp; and I saw the windows and balconies of the castle tower.

94. Drawing a small knife from my belt, I cut off both the eagle's feet.

95. The bird rose up in the air with a yelp, and I dropped lightly onto a broad balcony.

96. At the same moment a door opened, and I saw a courtyard filled with flowers and trees, and there, the beautiful enchanted symbol.

97. I approached the symbol, with its layers of meaning, but when I touched it, it changed into only a beautiful princess.

98. I threw the beautiful princess headfirst down the mountain to my acquaintances.

99. Who could be relied upon to deal with her.

100. Nor are eagles plausible, not at all, not for a moment.

I Bought a Little City

So I bought a little city (it was Galveston, Texas) and told everybody that nobody had to move, we were going to do it just gradually, very relaxed, no big changes overnight. They were pleased and suspicious. I walked down to the harbor where there were cotton warehouses and fish markets and all sorts of installations having to do with the spread of petroleum throughout the Free World, and I thought, A few apple trees here might be nice. Then I walked out on this broad boulevard which has all these tall thick palm trees maybe forty feet high in the center and oleanders on both sides, it runs for blocks and blocks and ends up opening up to the broad Gulf of Mexico – stately homes on both sides and a big Catholic church that looks more like a mosque and the Bishop's Palace and a handsome red brick affair where the Shriners meet. I thought, What a nice little city, it suits me fine.

It suited me fine so I started to change it. But softly,

softly. I asked some folks to move out of a whole city block on I Street, and then I tore down their houses. I put the people into the Galvez Hotel, which is the nicest hotel in town, right on the seawall, and I made sure that every room had a beautiful view. Those people had wanted to stay at the Galvez Hotel all their lives and never had a chance before because they didn't have the money. They were delighted. I tore down their houses and made that empty block a park. We planted it all to hell and put some nice green iron benches in it and a little fountain – all standard stuff, we didn't try to be imaginative.

I was pleased. All the people who lived in the four blocks surrounding the empty block had something they hadn't had before, a park. They could sit in it, and like that. I went and watched them sitting in it. There was already a black man there playing bongo drums. I hate bongo drums. I started to tell him to stop playing those goddamn bongo drums but then I said to myself, No, that's not right. You got to let him play his goddamn bongo drums if he feels like it, it's part of the misery of democracy, to which I subscribe. Then I started thinking about new housing for the people I had displaced, they couldn't stay in that fancy hotel forever.

But I didn't have any ideas about new housing, except that it shouldn't be too imaginative. So I got to talking to one of these people, one of the ones we had moved out, guy by the name of Bill Caulfield who worked in a wholesale-tobacco place down on Mechanic Street.

'So what kind of a place would you like to live in?' I asked him.

'Well,' he said, 'not too big.'

'Uh-huh.'

'Maybe with a veranda around three sides,' he said, 'so we could sit on it and look out. A screened porch, maybe.'

'Whatcha going to look out at?'

'Maybe some trees and, you know, the lawn.'

'So you want some ground around the house.'

'That would be nice, yeah.'

''Bout how much ground are you thinking of?'

'Well, not too much.'

'You see, the problem is, there's only x amount of ground and everybody's going to want to have it to look at and at the same time they don't want to be staring at the neighbors. Private looking, that's the thing.'

'Well, yes,' he said. 'I'd like it to be kind of private.'

'Well,' I said, 'get a pencil and let's see what we can work out.'

We started with what there was going to be to look at, which was damned difficult. Because when you look you don't want to be able to look at just one thing, you want to be able to shift your gaze. You need to be able to look at at least three things, maybe four. Bill Caulfield solved the problem. He showed me a box. I opened it up and inside was a jigsaw puzzle with a picture of the Mona Lisa on it.

'Lookee here,' he said. 'If each piece of ground was like a piece of this-here puzzle, and the tree line on each piece of property followed the outline of a piece of the puzzle – well, there you have it, QED and that's all she wrote.'

'Fine,' I said. 'Where are the folk going to park their cars?'

'In the vast underground parking facility,' he said.

'OK, but how does each householder gain access to his household?'

'The tree lines are double and shade beautifully paved walkways possibly bordered with begonias,' he said.

'A lurkway for potential muggists and rapers,' I pointed out.

'There won't be any such,' Caulfield said, 'because you've bought our whole city and won't allow that class of person to hang out here no more.'

That was right. I had bought the whole city and could probably do that. I had forgotten.

'Well,' I said finally, 'let's give 'er a try. The only thing I don't like about it is that it seems a little imaginative.'

We did and it didn't work out badly. There was only one complaint. A man named A. G. Bartie came to see me.

'Listen,' he said, his eyes either gleaming or burning, I couldn't tell which, it was a cloudy day, 'I feel like I'm living in this gigantic jiveass jigsaw puzzle.'

He was right. Seen from the air, he was living in the middle of a titanic reproduction of the Mona Lisa, too, but I thought it best not to mention that. We allowed him to square off his property into a standard 60 × 100 foot lot and later some other people did that too – some people just like rectangles, I guess. I must say it improved the concept. You run across an occasional rectangle in Shady Oaks (we didn't want to call the development anything too imaginative) and it surprises you. That's nice.

I said to myself:

> Got a little City
> Ain't it pretty

By now I had exercised my proprietorship so lightly and if I do say so myself tactfully that I wondered if I was enjoying myself enough (and I had paid a heavy penny too – near to half my fortune). So I went out on the streets then and shot six thousand dogs. This gave me great satisfaction and you have no idea how wonderfully it improved the city for the better. This left us with a dog population of 165,000, as opposed to a human population of something like 89,000. Then I went down to the Galveston *News*, the morning paper, and wrote an editorial denouncing myself as the vilest creature the good God had ever placed upon the earth, and were we, the citizens of this fine community, who were after all free Americans of whatever race or creed, going to sit still while one man, *one man*, if indeed so vile a critter could be so called, etc. etc.? I gave it to the city desk and told them I wanted it on the front page in fourteen-point type, boxed. I did this just in case they might have hesitated to do it themselves, and because I'd seen that Orson Welles picture where the guy writes a nasty notice about his own wife's terrible singing, which I always thought was pretty decent of him, from some points of view.

A man whose dog I'd shot came to see me.

'You shot Butch,' he said.

'Butch? Which one was Butch?'

'One brown ear and one white ear,' he said. 'Very friendly.'

'Mister,' I said, 'I've just shot six thousand dogs, and you expect me to remember Butch?'

'Butch was all Nancy and me had,' he said. 'We never had no children.'

'Well, I'm sorry about that,' I said, 'but I own this city.'

'I know that,' he said.

'I am the sole owner and I make all the rules.'

'They told me,' he said.

'I'm sorry about Butch but he got in the way of the big campaign. You ought to have had him on a leash.'

'I don't deny it,' he said.

'You ought to have had him inside the house.'

'He was just a poor animal that had to go out sometimes.'

'And mess up the streets something awful?'

'Well,' he said, 'it's a problem. I just wanted to tell you how I feel.'

'You didn't tell me,' I said. 'How do you feel?'

'I feel like bustin' your head,' he said, and showed me a short length of pipe he had brought along for the purpose.

'But of course if you do that you're going to get your ass in a lot of trouble,' I said.

'I realize that.'

'It would make you feel better, but then I own the jail and the judge and the po-lice and the local chapter of the American Civil Liberties Union. All mine. I could hit you with a writ of mandamus.'

'You wouldn't do that.'

'I've been known to do worse.'

'You're a black-hearted man,' he said. 'I guess that's

23

it. You'll roast in Hell in the eternal flames and there will be no mercy or cooling drafts from any quarter.'

He went away happy with this explanation. I was happy to be a black-hearted man in his mind if that would satisfy the issue between us because that was a bad-looking piece of pipe he had there and I was still six thousand dogs ahead of the game, in a sense. So I owned this little city which was very, very pretty and I couldn't think of any more new innovations just then or none that wouldn't get me punctuated like the late Huey P. Long, former governor of Louisiana. The thing is, I had fallen in love with Sam Hong's wife. I had wandered into this store on Tremont Street where they sold Oriental novelties, paper lanterns, and cheap china and bamboo birdcages and wicker footstools and all that kind of thing. She was smaller than I was and I thought I had never seen that much goodness in a woman's face before. It was hard to credit. It was the best face I'd ever seen.

'I can't do that,' she said, 'because I am married to Sam.'

'Sam?'

She pointed over to the cash register where there was a Chinese man, young and intelligent-looking and pouring that intelligent look at me with considered unfriendliness.

'Well, that's dismal news,' I said. 'Tell me, do you love me?'

'A little bit,' she said, 'but Sam is wise and kind and we have one and one-third lovely children.'

She didn't look pregnant but I congratulated her anyhow, and then went out on the street and found a cop and sent him down to H Street to get me a bucket of Colonel Sanders' Kentucky Fried Chicken, extra crispy. I did that just out of meanness. He was humiliated but he had no choice. I thought:

> I own a little city
> Awful pretty
> Can't help people
> Can hurt them though
> Shoot their dogs
> Mess 'em up
> Be imaginative
> Plant trees
> Best to leave 'em alone?
> Who decides?
> Sam's wife is Sam's wife and coveting
> Is not nice.

So I ate the Colonel Sanders' Kentucky Fried Chicken, extra crispy, and sold Galveston, Texas, back to the interests. I took a bath on that deal, there's no denying it, but I learned something – don't play God. A lot of other people already knew that, but I have never doubted for a minute that a lot of other people are smarter than me, and figure things out quicker, and have grace and statistical norms on their side. Probably I went wrong by being too imaginative, although really I was guarding against that. I did very little, I was fairly restrained. God does a lot worse things, every day, in one little family, any family, than I did in that whole city. But He's got a better imagination than I do. For instance, I still covet Sam Hong's wife. That's torment. Still covet Sam Hong's wife, and probably always will. It's like having a tooth pulled. For a year. The same tooth. That's a sample of His imagination. It's powerful.

So what happened? What happened was that I took the other half of my fortune and went to Galena Park, Texas, and lived inconspicuously there, and when they asked me to run for the school board I said No, I don't have any children.

The Palace at Four A.M.

My father's kingdom was and is, all authorities agree, large. To walk border to border east-west, the traveler must budget no less than seventeen days. Its name is Ho, the Confucian term for harmony. Confucianism was an interest of the first ruler (a strange taste in our part of the world), and when he'd cleared his expanse of field and forest of his enemies, two centuries ago, he indulged himself in an *hommage* to the great Chinese thinker, much to the merriment of some of our staider neighbors, whose domains were proper Luftlunds and Dolphinlunds. We have an economy based upon truffles, in which our forests are spectacularly rich, and electricity, which we were exporting when other countries still read by kerosene lamp. Our army is the best in the region, every man a colonel – the subtle secret of my father's rule, if the truth be known. In this land every priest is a bishop, every ambulance-chaser a robed justice, every peasant a corporation and every street-corner

shouter Hegel himself. My father's genius was to pro-
mote his subjects, male and female, across the board,
ceaselessly; the people of Ho warm themselves forever
in the sun of Achievement. I was the only man in the
kingdom who thought himself a donkey.

– From the *Autobiography*

I am writing to you, Hannahbella, from a distant country. I daresay you remember it well. The King encloses
the opening pages of his autobiography. He is most
curious as to what your response to them will be. He
has labored mightily over their composition, working
without food, without sleep, for many days and nights.

The King has not been, in these months, in the best
of spirits. He has read your article and declares himself
to be very much impressed by it. He begs you, prior to
publication in this country, to do him the great favor of
changing the phrase 'two disinterested and impartial
arbiters' on page thirty-one to 'malign elements under
the ideological sway of still more malign elements.'
Otherwise, he is delighted. He asks me to tell you that
your touch is as adroit as ever.

Early in the autobiography (as you see) we encounter
the words: 'My mother the Queen made a mirror pie, a
splendid thing the size of a poker table . . .' The King
wishes to know if poker tables are in use in faraway

lands, and whether the reader in such places would com-
prehend the dimensions of the pie. He continues: '. . . in
which reflections from the kitchen chandelier exploded
when the crew rolled it from the oven. We were kneeling
side-by-side, peering into the depths of a new-made mirror pie, when my mother said to me, or rather her celestial
image said to my dark, heavy-haired one, "Get out. I cannot bear to look upon your donkey face again."'

The King wishes to know, Hannahbella, whether this
passage seems to you tainted by self-pity, or is, rather,
suitably dispassionate.

He walks up and down the small room next to his
bedchamber, singing your praises. The decree having to
do with your banishment will be rescinded, he says, the
moment you agree to change the phrase 'two disinterested and impartial arbiters' to 'malign elements,' etc.
This I urge you to do with all speed.

The King has not been at his best. Peace, he says, is
an unnatural condition. The country is prosperous, yes,
and he understands that the people value peace, that
they prefer to spin out their destinies in placid, undis-
turbed fashion. But *his* destiny, he says, is to alter the
map of the world. He is considering several new wars,
small ones, he says, small but interesting, complex, dicey,
even. He would very much like to consult with you
about them. He asks you to change, on page forty-four

of your article, the phrase 'egregious usurpations' to 'symbols of benign transformation.' Please initial the change on the proofs, so that historians will not accuse us of bowdlerization.

Your attention is called to the passage in the pages I send which runs as follows: 'I walked out of the castle at dusk, not even the joy of a new sunrise to console me, my shaving kit with its dozen razors (although I shaved a dozen times a day, the head was still a donkey's) banging against the Walther .22 in my rucksack. After a time I was suddenly quite tired. I lay down under a hedge by the side of the road. One of the bushes above me had a shred of black cloth tied to it, a sign, in our country, that the place was haunted (but my head's enough to frighten any ghost).' Do you remember that shred of black cloth, Hannahbella? 'I ate a slice of my mother's spinach pie and considered my situation. My princeliness would win me an evening, perhaps a fortnight, at this or that noble's castle in the vicinity, but my experience of visiting had taught me that neither royal blood nor novelty of aspect prevailed for long against a host's natural preference for folk with heads much like his own. Should I en-zoo myself? Volunteer for a traveling circus? Attempt the stage? The question was most vexing.

'I had not wiped the last crumbs of the spinach pie

from my whiskers when something lay down beside me, under the hedge.

' "What's this?" I said.

' "Soft," said the new arrival, "don't be afraid, I am a bogle, let me abide here for the night, your back is warm and that's a mercy."

' "What's a bogle?" I asked, immediately fetched, for the creature was small, not at all frightening to look upon and clad in female flesh, something I do not hold in low esteem.

' "A bogle," said the tiny one, with precision, "is not a black dog."

'Well, I thought, now I know.

' "A bogle," she continued, "is not a boggart."

' "Delighted to hear it," I said.

"Don't you ever *shave*?" she asked. "And why have you that huge hideous head on you, that could be mistaken for the head of an ass, could I see better so as to think better?"

' "You may lie elsewhere," I said, "if my face discountenances you."

' "I am fatigued," she said, "go to sleep, we'll discuss it in the morning, move a bit so that your back fits better with my front, it will be cold, later, and this place is cursed, so they say, and I hear that the Prince has been driven from the palace, God knows what that's all about

31

but it promises no good for us plain folk, police, probably, running all over the fens with their identity checks
and making you blow up their great balloons with your
breath –"

'She was confusing, I thought, several issues, but my
God! she was warm and shapely. Yet I thought her a
strange piece of goods, and made the mistake of saying so.

'"Sir," she answered, "I would not venture upon
what's strange and what's not strange, if I were you,"
and went on to say that if I did not abstain from further
impertinence she would commit sewer-pipe. She
dropped off to sleep then, and I lay back upon the
ground. Not a child, I could tell, rather a tiny woman. A
bogle.'

The King wishes you to know, Hannahbella, that he
finds this passage singularly moving and that he cannot
read it without being forced to take snuff, violently.
Similarly the next:

'What, precisely, is a donkey? As you may imagine, I
have researched the question. My *Larousse* was most
delicate, as if the editors thought the matter blushful,
but yielded two observations of interest: that donkeys
came originally from Africa, and that they, or we, are
"the result of much crossing." This urges that the par-
ties to the birth must be ill-matched, and in the case of

my royal parents, twas thunderously true. The din of their calamitous conversations reached every quarter of the palace, at every season of the year. My mother named me Duncan (var. of Dunkey, clearly) and went into spasms of shrinking whenever, youthfully, I'd offer a cheek for a kiss. My father, in contrast, could sometimes bring himself to scratch my head between the long, weedlike ears, but only, I suspect, by means of a mental shift, as if he were addressing one of his hunting dogs, the which, incidentally, remained firmly ambivalent about me even after long acquaintance.

'I explained a part of this to Hannahbella, for that was the bogle's name, suppressing chiefly the fact that I was a prince. She in turn gave the following account of herself. She was indeed a bogle, a semispirit generally thought to be of bad character. This was a libel, she said, as her own sterling qualities would quickly persuade me. She was, she said, of the utmost perfection in the female line, and there was not a woman within the borders of the kingdom so beautiful as herself, she'd been told it a thousand times. It was true, she went on, that she was not of a standard size, could in fact be called small, if not minuscule, but those who objected to this were louts and fools and might profitably be stewed in lead, for the entertainment of the countryside. In the matter of rank and precedence, the meanest bogle outweighed the greatest king, although the kings of this earth, she conceded, would never acknowledge this but in their dotty solipsism conducted themselves as if bogles did not even exist. And would I like to see her all unclothed so that I might glean some rude idea as to the true nature of the sublime?

'Well, I wouldn't have minded a bit. She was wonderfully crafted, that was evident, and held in addition the fascination surrounding any perfect miniature. But I said, 'No, thank you. Perhaps another day, it's a bit chill this morning.'

'"Just the breasts then," she said, "they're wondrous pretty," and before I could protest further she'd whipped off her mannikin's tiny shirt. I buttoned her up again meanwhile bestowing buckets of extravagant praise. "Yes," she said in agreement, "that's how I am all over, wonderful."'

The King cannot reread this section, Hannahbella, without being reduced to tears. The world is a wilderness, he says, civilization a folly we entertain in concert with others. He himself, at his age, is beyond surprise, yet yearns for it. He longs for the conversations he formerly had with you, in the deepest hours of the night, he in his plain ermine robe, you simply dressed as always in a small scarlet cassock, most becoming, a modest supper of chicken, fruit and wine on the sideboard, only the pair of you awake in the whole palace, at four o'clock in the morning. The tax evasion case against you has been dropped. It was, he says, a hasty and ill-considered undertaking, even spiteful. He is sorry.

The King wonders whether the following paragraphs from his autobiography accord with your own recollections: 'She then began, as we walked down the road together (an owl pretending to be absent standing on a tree limb to our left, a little stream snapping and growling to our right), explaining to me that my father's administration of the realm left much to be desired, from the bogle point of view, particularly his mad insistence on filling the forests with heavy-footed truffle hounds. Standing, she came to just a hand above my waist; her hair was brown, with bits of gold in it; her quite womanly hips were encased in dun-colored trousers. "Duncan," she said, stabbing me in the calf with her sharp nails, "do you know what that man has done? Nothing else but ruin, absolutely ruin, the whole of the Gatter Fen with a great roaring electric plant that makes a thing that who in the world could have a use for I don't know. I think they're called volts. Two square miles of first-class fen paved over. We bogles are being squeezed to our knees." I had a sudden urge to kiss her, she looked so angry, but did nothing, my history in this regard being, as I have said, infelicitous.

' "Duncan, *you're not listening!*" Hannahbella was naming the chief interesting things about bogles, which included the fact that in the main they had nothing to do with humans, or nonsemispirits; that although she might seem small to me she was tall, for a bogle, queenly, in fact; that there was a type of blood seas superior to royal blood, and that it was bogle blood; that bogles had no magical powers whatsoever, despite what was said of them; that bogles were the very best lovers in the whole world, no matter what class of thing, animal, vegetable, or insect, might be under discussion; that it was not true that bogles knocked bowls of mush from the tables of the deserving poor and caused farmers' cows to become pregnant with big fishes, out of pure mischief; that female bogles were the most satisfactory sexual partners of any kind of thing that could ever be imagined and were especially keen for large overgrown things with ass's ears, for example; and that there was a something in the road ahead of us to which it might, perhaps, be prudent to pay heed.

She was right. One hundred yards ahead of us, planted squarely athwart the road, was an army.

The King, Hannahbella, regrets having said of you, in the journal *Vu*, that you have two brains and no heart. He had thought he was talking not-for-attribution, but as you know, all reporters are scoundrels and not to be trusted. He asks you to note that *Vu* has suspended publication and to recall that it was never read by anyone but serving maids and the most insignificant members of the minor clergy. He is prepared to give you a medal, if you return, any medal you like – you will remember that our medals are the most gorgeous going. On page seventy-five of your article, he requires you, most humbly, to change 'monstrous over-reaching fueled by an insatiable if still childish ego' to any kinder construction of your choosing.

The King's autobiography, in chapters already written but which I do not enclose, goes on to recount how you and he together, by means of a clever stratagem of your devising, vanquished the army barring your path on that day long, long ago; how the two of you journeyed together for many weeks and found that your souls were, in essence, the same soul; the shrewd means you employed to place him in power, against the armed opposition of the Party of the Lily, on the death of his father; and the many subsequent campaigns which you endured together, mounted on a single horse, your armor banging against his armor. The King's autobiography, Hannahbella, will run to many volumes, but he cannot bring himself to write the end of the story without you.

The King feels that your falling-out, over the matter

Donald Barthelme

of the refugees from Brise, was the result of a miscalculation on his part. He could not have known, he says, that they had bogle blood (although he admits that the fact of their small stature should have told him something). Exchanging the refugees from Brise for the twenty-three Bishops of Ho captured during the affair was, he says in hindsight, a serious error; more bishops can always be created. He makes the point that you did not tell him that the refugees from Brise had bogle blood but instead expected him to know it. Your outrage was, he thinks, a pretext. He at once forgives you and begs your forgiveness. The Chair of Military Philosophy at the university is yours, if you want it. You loved him, he says, he is convinced of it, he still cannot believe it, he exists in a condition of doubt. You are both old; you are both forty. The palace at four A.M. is silent. Come back, Hannahbella, and speak to him.

Chablis

My wife wants a dog. She already has a baby. The baby's
almost two. My wife says that the baby wants the dog.

My wife has been wanting a dog for a long time. I
have had to be the one to tell her that she couldn't have
it. But now the baby wants a dog, my wife says. This
may be true. The baby is very close to my wife. They go
around together all the time, clutching each other tightly.
I ask the baby, who is a girl, 'Whose girl are you? Are you
Daddy's girl?' The baby says, 'Momma,' and she doesn't
just say it once, she says it repeatedly, 'Momma momma
momma.' I don't see why I should buy a hundred-dollar
dog for that damn baby.

The kind of dog the baby wants, my wife says, is a
Cairn terrier. This kind of dog, my wife says, is a Presbyterian like herself and the baby. Last year the baby
was a Baptist – that is, she went to the Mother's Day
Out program at the First Baptist twice a week. This
year she is a Presbyterian because the Presbyterians

39

have more swings and slides and things. I think that's pretty shameless and I have said so. My wife is a legitimate lifelong Presbyterian and says that makes it O.K.; way back when she was a child she used to go to the First Presbyterian in Evansville, Illinois. I didn't go to church because I was a black sheep. There were five children in my family and the males rotated the position of black sheep among us, the oldest one being the black sheep for a while while he was in his DWI period or whatever and then getting grayer as he maybe got a job or was in the service and then finally becoming a white sheep when he got married and had a grandchild. My sister was never a black sheep because she was a girl.

Our baby is a pretty fine baby. I told my wife for many years that she couldn't have a baby because it was too expensive. But they wear you down. They are just wonderful at wearing you down, even if it takes years, as it did in this case. Now I hang around the baby and hug her every chance I get. Her name is Joanna. She wears Oshkosh overalls and says 'no,' 'bottle,' 'out,' and 'Momma.' She looks most lovable when she's wet, when she's just had a bath and her blond hair is all wet and she's wrapped in a beige towel. Sometimes when she's watching television she forgets that you're there. You can just look at her. When she's watching television, she looks dumb. I like her better when she's wet.

This dog thing is getting to be a big issue. I said to my wife, 'Well you've got the baby, do we have to have the damned dog too?' The dog will probably bite somebody, or get lost. I can see myself walking all over our subdivision asking people, 'Have you seen this brown dog?' 'What's its name?' they'll say to me, and I'll stare at them coldly and say, 'Michael.' That's what she wants to call it, Michael. That's a silly name for a dog and I'll have to go looking for this possibly rabid animal and say to people, 'Have you seen this brown dog? Michael?' It's enough to make you think about divorce.

What's that baby going to do with that dog that it can't do with me? Romp? I can romp. I took her to the playground at the school. It was Sunday and there was nobody there, and we romped. I ran, and she tottered after me at a good pace. I held her as she slid down the slide. She groped her way through a length of big pipe they have there set in concrete. She picked up a feather and looked at it for a long time. I was worried that it might be a diseased feather but she didn't put it in her mouth. Then we ran some more over the parched bare softball field and through the arcade that connects the temporary wooden classrooms, which are losing their yellow paint, to the main building. Joanna will go to this school some day, if I stay in the same job.

I looked at some dogs at Pets-A-Plenty, which has

41

birds, rodents, reptiles, and dogs, all in top condition. They showed me the Cairn terriers. 'Do they have their prayer books?' I asked. This woman clerk didn't know what I was talking about. The Cairn terriers ran about two ninety-five per, with their papers. I started to ask if they had any illegitimate children at lower prices but I could see that it would be useless and the woman already didn't like me, I could tell.

What is wrong with me? Why am I not a more natural person, like my wife wants me to be? I sit up, in the early morning, at my desk on the second floor of our house. The desk faces the street. At five-thirty in the morning, the runners are already out, individually or in pairs, running toward rude red health. I'm sipping a glass of Gallo Chablis with an ice cube in it, smoking, worrying. I worry that the baby may jam a kitchen knife into an electrical outlet while she's wet. I've put those little plastic plugs into all the electrical outlets but she's learned how to pop them out. I've checked the Crayolas. They've made the Crayolas safe to eat – I called the head office in Pennsylvania. She can eat a whole box of Crayolas and nothing will happen to her. If I don't get the new tires for the car I can buy the dog.

I remember the time, thirty years ago, when I put Herman's mother's Buick into a cornfield, on the Beaumont highway. There was another car in my lane, and I didn't hit it, and it didn't hit me. I remember veering to the right and down into the ditch and up through the fence and coming to rest in the cornfield and then getting out to wake Herman and the two of us going to see what the happy drunks in the other car had come to, in the ditch on the other side of the road. That was when I was a black sheep, years and years ago. That was skillfully done, I think. I get up, congratulate myself in memory, and go in to look at the baby.

The School

Well, we had all these children out planting trees, see, because we figured that . . . that was part of their education, to see how, you know, the root systems . . . and also the sense of responsibility, taking care of things, being individually responsible. You know what I mean. And the trees all died. They were orange trees. I don't know why they died, they just died. Something wrong with the soil possibly or maybe the stuff we got from the nursery wasn't the best. We complained about it. So we've got thirty kids there, each kid had his or her own little tree to plant, and we've got these thirty dead trees. All these kids looking at these little brown sticks, it was depressing.

It wouldn't have been so bad except that just a couple of weeks before the thing with the trees, the snakes all died. But I think that the snakes – well, the reason that the snakes kicked off was that . . . you remember, the boiler was shut off for four days because of the strike,

Donald Barthelme

and that was explicable. It was something you could explain to the kids because of the strike. I mean, none of their parents would let them cross the picket line and they knew there was a strike going on and what it meant. So when things got started up again and we found the snakes they weren't too disturbed.

With the herb gardens it was probably a case of over-watering, and at least now they know not to overwater. The children were very conscientious with the herb gardens and some of them probably . . . you know, slipped them a little extra water when we weren't looking. Or maybe . . . well, I don't like to think about sabotage, although it did occur to us. I mean, it was something that crossed our minds. We were thinking that way probably because before that the gerbils had died, and the white mice had died, and the salamander . . . well, now they know not to carry them around in plastic bags.

Of course we *expected* the tropical fish to die, that was no surprise. Those numbers, you look at them crooked and they're belly-up on the surface. But the lesson plan called for a tropical-fish input at that point, there was nothing we could do, it happens every year, you just have to hurry past it.

We weren't even supposed to have a puppy.

We weren't even supposed to have one, it was just a puppy the Murdoch girl found under a Gristede's truck

46

one day and she was afraid the truck would run over it when the driver had finished making his delivery, so she stuck it in her knapsack and brought it to school with her. So we had this puppy. As soon as I saw the puppy I thought, Oh Christ, I bet it will live for about two weeks and then . . . And that's what it did. It wasn't supposed to be in the classroom at all, there's some kind of regulation about it, but you can't tell them they can't have a puppy when the puppy is already there, right in front of them, running around on the floor and yap yap yapping. They named it Edgar – that is, they named it after me. They had a lot of fun running after it and yelling, 'Here, Edgar! Nice Edgar!' Then they'd laugh like hell. They enjoyed the ambiguity. I enjoyed it myself. I don't mind being kidded. They made a little house for it in the supply closet and all that. I don't know what it died of. Distemper, I guess. It probably hadn't had any shots. I got it out of there before the kids got to school. I checked the supply closet each morning, routinely, because I knew what was going to happen. I gave it to the custodian.

And then there was this Korean orphan that the class adopted through the Help the Children program, all the kids brought in a quarter a month, that was the idea. It was an unfortunate thing, the kid's name was Kim and maybe we adopted him too late or something. The cause of death was not stated in the letter we got, they suggested we adopt another child instead and sent us some interesting case histories, but we didn't have the heart. The class took it pretty hard, they began (I think; nobody ever said anything to me directly) to feel that maybe there was something wrong with the school. But I don't think there's anything wrong with the school, particularly, I've seen better and I've seen worse. It was just a run of bad luck. We had an extraordinary number of parents passing away, for instance. There were I think two heart attacks and two suicides, one drowning, and four killed together in a car accident. One stroke. And we had the usual heavy mortality rate among the grandparents, or maybe it was heavier this year, it seemed so. And finally the tragedy.

The tragedy occurred when Matthew Wein and Tony Mavrogordo were playing over where they're excavating for the new federal office building. There were all these big wooden beams stacked, you know, at the edge of the excavation. There's a court case coming out of that, the parents are claiming that the beams were poorly stacked. I don't know what's true and what's not. It's been a strange year.

I forgot to mention Billy Brandt's father, who was knifed fatally when he grappled with a masked intruder in his home.

One day, we had a discussion in class. They asked

me, where did they go? The trees, the salamander, the tropical fish, Edgar, the poppas and mommas, Matthew and Tony, where did they go? And I said, I don't know, I don't know. And they said, who knows? and I said, nobody knows. And they said, is death that which gives meaning to life? And I said, no, life is that which gives meaning to life. Then they said, but isn't death, considered as a fundamental datum, the means by which the taken-for-granted mundanity of the everyday may be transcended in the direction of –

I said, yes, maybe.

They said, we don't like it.

I said, that's sound.

They said, it's a bloody shame!

I said, it is.

They said, will you make love now with Helen (our teaching assistant) so that we can see how it is done? We know you like Helen.

I do like Helen but I said that I would not.

We've heard so much about it, they said, but we've never seen it.

I said I would be fired and that it was never, or almost never, done as a demonstration. Helen looked out of the window.

They said, please, please make love with Helen, we require an assertion of value, we are frightened.

I said that they shouldn't be frightened (although I am often frightened) and that there was value everywhere. Helen came and embraced me. I kissed her a few times on the brow. We held each other. The children were excited. Then there was a knock on the door, I opened the door, and the new gerbil walked in. The children cheered wildly.

Margins

Edward was explaining to Carl about margins. 'The *width* of the margin shows culture, aestheticism and a sense of values or the lack of them,' he said. 'A very wide left margin shows an impractical person of culture and refinement with a deep appreciation for the best in art and music. Whereas,' Edward said, quoting his handwriting analysis book, 'whereas, narrow left margins show the opposite. No left margin at all shows a practical nature, a wholesome economy and a general lack of good taste in the arts. A very wide *right* margin shows a person afraid to face reality, oversensitive to the future and generally a poor mixer.'

'I don't believe in it,' Carl said.

'Now,' Edward continued, 'with reference to your sign there, you have an *all-around wide margin* which shows a person of extremely delicate sensibilities with love of color and form, one who holds aloof from the multitude and lives in his own dream world of beauty and good taste.'

'Are you sure you got that right?'

'I'm communicating with you,' Edward said, 'across a vast gulf of ignorance and darkness.'

'*I* brought the darkness, is that the idea?' Carl asked.

'You brought the darkness, you black mother,' Edward said. 'Funky, man.'

'Edward,' Carl said, 'for God's sake.'

'Why did you write all that jazz on your sign, Carl? Why? It's not true, is it? Is it?'

'It's kind of true,' Carl said. He looked down at his brown sandwich boards, which said: *I Was Put In Jail in Selby County Alabama For Five Years For Stealing A Dollar and A Half Which I Did Not Do. While I Was In Jail My Brother Was Killed & My Mother Ran Away When I Was Little. In Jail I Began Preaching & I Preach to People Wherever I Can Bearing the Witness of Eschatological Love. I Have Filled Out Papers for Jobs But Nobody Will Give Me a Job Because I Have Been In Jail & The Whole Scene Is Very Dreary, Pepsi Cola. I Need Your Offerings to Get Food. Patent Applied For & Deliver Us From Evil.* 'It's true,' Carl said, 'with a kind of *merde*-y inner truth which shines forth as the objective correlative of what actually did happen, back home.'

'Now, look at the way you made that "m" and that "n" there,' Edward said. 'The tops are pointed rather than rounded. That indicates aggressiveness and energy. The fact that they're also pointed rather than rounded at the bottom indicates a sarcastic, stubborn and irritable nature. See what I mean?'

'If you say so,' Carl said.

'Your capitals are very small,' Edward said, 'indicating humility.'

'My mother would be pleased,' Carl said, 'if she knew.'

'On the other hand, the excessive size of the loops in your "y" and your "g" displays exaggeration and egoism.'

'That's always been one of my problems,' Carl answered.

'What's your whole name?' Edward asked, leaning against a building. They were on Fourteenth Street, near Broadway.

'Carl Maria von Weber,' Carl said.

'Are you a drug addict?'

'Edward,' Carl said, 'you *are* a swinger.'

'Are you a Muslim?'

Carl felt his long hair. 'Have you read *As a Man Grows Older*, by Svevo? I really liked that one. I thought that one was fine.'

'No, c'mon, Carl, answer the question,' Edward insisted. 'There's got to be frankness and honesty between the races. Are you one?'

'I think an accommodation can be reached and the government is doing all it can at the moment,' Carl said. 'I think there's something to be said on all sides of the question. This is not such a good place to hustle, you know that? I haven't got but two offerings all morning.'

'People like people who look neat,' Edward said. 'You look kind of crummy, if you don't mind my saying so.'

'You really think it's too long?' Carl asked, feeling his hair again.

'Do you think I'm a pretty color?' Edward asked. 'Are you envious?'

'No,' Carl said. 'Not envious.'

'See? Exaggeration and egoism. Just like I said.'

'You're kind of boring, Edward. To tell the truth.'

Edward thought about this for a moment. Then he said: 'But I'm white.'

'It's the color of choice,' Carl said. 'I'm tired of talking about color, though. Let's talk about values or something.'

'Carl, I'm a fool,' Edward said suddenly.

'Yes,' Carl said.

'But I'm a *white* fool,' Edward said. 'That's what's so lovely about me.'

'You *are* lovely, Edward,' Carl said. 'It's true. You have a nice look. Your aspect is good.'

'Oh, hell,' Edward said despondently. 'You're very well-spoken,' he said. 'I noticed that.'

'The reason for that is,' Carl said, 'I read. Did you read *The Cannibal* by John Hawkes? I thought that was a hell of a book.'

'Get a haircut, Carl,' Edward said. 'Get a new suit. Maybe one of those new Italian suits with the tight coats. You could be upwardly mobile, you know, if you just put your back into it.'

'Why are you worried, Edward? Why does my situation distress you? Why don't you just walk away and talk to somebody else?'

'You bother me,' Edward confessed. 'I keep trying to penetrate your inner reality, to find out what it is. Isn't that curious?'

'John Hawkes also wrote *The Beetle Leg* and a couple of other books whose titles escape me at the moment,' Carl said. 'I think he's one of the best of our younger American writers.'

'Carl,' Edward said, '*what* is your inner reality? Blurt it out, baby.'

'It's mine,' Carl said quietly. He gazed down at his shoes, which resembled a pair of large dead brownish birds.

'Are you sure you didn't steal that dollar and a half mentioned on your sign?'

'Edward, I *told* you I didn't steal that dollar and a half.' Carl stamped up and down in his sandwich boards. 'It sure is *cold* here on Fourteenth Street.'

'That's your imagination, Carl,' Edward said. 'This street isn't any colder than Fifth, or Lex. Your feeling that it's colder here probably just arises from your marginal status as a despised person in our society.'

'Probably,' Carl said. There was a look on his face. 'You know I went to the government, and asked them to give me a job in the Marine Band, and they wouldn't do it?'

'Do you blow good, man? Where's your ax?'

'They wouldn't *give* me that cotton-pickin' job,' Carl said. 'What do you think of that?'

'This eschatological love,' Edward said, 'what kind of love is that?'

'That is later love,' Carl said. 'That's what I call it, anyhow. That's love on the other side of the Jordan. The term refers to a set of conditions which . . . It's kind of a story we black people tell to ourselves to make ourselves happy.'

'Oh me,' Edward said. 'Ignorance and darkness.'

'Edward,' Carl said, 'you don't *like* me.'

'I do too like you, Carl,' Edward said. 'Where do you steal your books, mostly?'

'Mostly in drugstores,' Carl said. 'I find them good because mostly they're long and narrow and the clerks tend to stay near the prescription counters at the back of the store, whereas the books are usually in those little revolving racks near the front of the store. It's normally pretty easy to slip a couple in your overcoat pocket, if you're wearing an overcoat.'

'But . . .'

'Yes,' Carl said, 'I know what you're thinking. If I'll steal books I'll steal other things. But stealing books is metaphysically different from stealing like money. Villon has something pretty good to say on the subject I believe.'

'Is that in "If I Were King"?'

'Besides,' Carl added, 'haven't *you* ever stolen anything? At some point in your life?'

'My life,' Edward said. 'Why do you remind me of it?'

'Edward, you're not satisfied with your life! I thought white lives were *nice!*' Carl said, surprised. 'I love that word "nice." It makes me so happy.'

'Listen Carl,' Edward said, 'why don't you just concentrate on improving your handwriting.'

'My character, you mean.'

'No,' Edward said, 'don't bother improving your character. Just improve your handwriting. Make larger capitals. Make smaller loops in your "y" and your "g." Watch your word-spacing so as not to display disorientation. Watch your margins.'

'It's an idea. But isn't that kind of a superficial approach to the problem?'

'Be careful about the spaces between the lines,' Edward went on. 'Spacing of lines shows clearness of thought. Pay attention to your finals. There are twenty-two different kinds of finals and each one tells a lot about a person. I'll lend you the book. Good handwriting is the key to advancement, or if not *the* key, at least *a* key. You could be the first man of your race to be Vice-President.'

'That's something to shoot for, all right.'

'Would you like me to go get the book?'

'I don't think so,' Carl said, 'no thanks. It's not that I don't have any faith in your solution. What I *would* like is to take a leak. Would you mind holding my sandwich boards for a minute?'

'Not at all,' Edward said, and in a moment had slipped Carl's sandwich boards over his own slight shoulders. 'Boy, they're kind of heavy, aren't they?'

'They cut you a bit,' Carl said with a malicious smile. 'I'll just go into this men's store here.'

When Carl returned the two men slapped each other sharply in the face with the back of the hand – that beautiful part of the hand where the knuckles grow.

Game

Shotwell keeps the jacks and the rubber ball in his attaché case and will not allow me to play with them. He plays with them, alone, sitting on the floor near the console hour after hour, chanting 'onesies, twosies, threesies, foursies' in a precise, well-modulated voice, not so loud as to be annoying, not so soft as to allow me to forget. I point out to Shotwell that two can derive more enjoyment from playing jacks than one, but he is not interested. I have asked repeatedly to be allowed to play by myself, but he simply shakes his head. 'Why?' I ask. 'They're mine,' he says. And when he has finished, when he has sated himself, back they go into the attaché case.

It is unfair but there is nothing I can do about it. I am aching to get my hands on them.

Shotwell and I watch the console. Shotwell and I live under the ground and watch the console. If certain events take place upon the console, we are to insert our keys in the appropriate locks and turn our keys. Shotwell has a key and I have a key. If we turn our keys simultaneously the bird flies, certain switches are activated and the bird flies. But the bird never flies. In one hundred thirty-three days the bird has not flown. Meanwhile Shotwell and I watch each other. We each wear a .45 and if Shotwell behaves strangely I am supposed to shoot him. If I behave strangely Shotwell is supposed to shoot me. We watch the console and think about shooting each other and think about the bird. Shotwell's behavior with the jacks is strange. Is it strange? I do not know. Perhaps he is merely a selfish bastard, perhaps his character is flawed, perhaps his childhood was twisted. I do not know.

Each of us wears a .45 and each of us is supposed to shoot the other if the other is behaving strangely. How strangely is strangely? I do not know. In addition to the .45 I have a .38 which Shotwell does not know about concealed in my attaché case, and Shotwell has a .25 caliber Beretta which I do not know about strapped to his right calf. Sometimes instead of watching the console I pointedly watch Shotwell's .45, but this is simply a ruse, simply a maneuver, in reality I am watching his hand when it dangles in the vicinity of his right calf. If he decides I am behaving strangely he will shoot me not with the .45 but with the Beretta. Similarly Shotwell pretends to watch my .45 but he is really watching my hand resting idly atop my attaché case, my hand resting idly atop my attaché case, my hand. My hand resting idly atop my attaché case.

In the beginning I took care to behave normally. So did Shotwell. Our behavior was painfully normal. Norms of politeness, consideration, speech, and personal habits were scrupulously observed. But then it became apparent that an error had been made, that our relief was not going to arrive. Owing to an oversight. Owing to an oversight we have been here for one hundred thirty-three days. When it became clear that an error had been made, that we were not to be relieved, the norms were relaxed. Definitions of normality were redrawn in the agreement of January 1, called by us, The Agreement. Uniform regulations were relaxed, and mealtimes are no longer rigorously scheduled. We eat when we are hungry and sleep when we are tired. Considerations of rank and precedence were temporarily put aside, a handsome concession on the part of Shotwell, who is a captain, whereas I am only a first lieutenant. One of us watches the console at all times rather than two of us watching the console at all times, except when we are both on our feet. One of us watches the console at all times and if the bird flies then that one wakes the other and we turn our keys in the locks simultaneously and the bird flies. Our system involves a delay of perhaps twelve seconds but I do not care because I am not well, and Shotwell does not care because he is not himself. After the agreement was signed Shotwell produced the jacks and the rubber ball from his attaché case, and I began to write a series of descriptions of forms occurring in nature, such as a shell, a leaf, a stone, an animal. On the walls.

Shotwell plays jack and I write descriptions of natural forms on the walls.

Shotwell is enrolled in a USAFI course which leads to a master's degree in business administration from the University of Wisconsin (although we are not in Wisconsin, we are in Utah, Montana or Idaho). When we went down it was in either Utah, Montana or Idaho, I don't remember. We have been here for one hundred thirty-three days owing to an oversight. The pale-green reinforced concrete walls sweat and the air conditioning zips on and off erratically and Shotwell reads *Introduction to Marketing* by Lassiter and Munk, making notes with a blue ballpoint pen. Shotwell is not himself, but I do not know it, he presents a calm aspect and reads *Introduction to Marketing* and makes his exemplary notes with a blue ballpoint pen, meanwhile controlling the .38 in my attaché case with one-third of his attention. I am not well.

We have been here one hundred thirty-three days

owing to an oversight. Although now we are not sure what is oversight, what is plan. Perhaps the plan is for us to stay here permanently, or if not permanently at least for a year, for three hundred sixty-five days. Or if not for a year for some number of days known to them and not known to us, such as two hundred days. Or perhaps they are observing our behavior in some way, sensors of some kind, perhaps our behavior determines the number of days. It may be that they are pleased with us, with our behavior, not in every detail but in sum. Perhaps the whole thing is very successful, perhaps the whole thing is an experiment and the experiment is very successful. I do not know. But I suspect that the only way they can persuade sunloving creatures into their pale green sweating reinforced concrete rooms under the ground is to say that the system is twelve hours on, twelve hours off. And then lock us below for some number of days known to them and not known to us. We eat well although the frozen enchiladas are damp when defrosted and the frozen devil's food cake is sour and untasty. We sleep uneasily and acrimoniously. I hear Shotwell shouting in his sleep, objecting, denouncing, cursing sometimes, weeping sometimes, in his sleep. When Shotwell sleeps I try to pick the lock on his attaché case, so as to get at the jacks. Thus far I have been unsuccessful. Nor has Shotwell been successful in picking the locks on my attaché case so as to get at the .38. I have seen the marks on the shiny surface. I laughed, in the latrine, pale green walls sweating and the air conditioning whispering, in the latrine.

I write descriptions of natural forms on the walls, scratching them on the tile surface with a diamond. The diamond is a two and one-half carat solitaire I had in my attaché case when we went down. It was for Lucy. The south wall of the room containing the console is already covered. I have described a shell, a leaf, a stone, animals, a baseball bat. I am aware that the baseball bat is not a natural form. Yet I described it. 'The baseball bat,' I said, 'is typically made of wood. It is typically one meter in length or a little longer, fat at one end, tapering to afford a comfortable grip at the other. The end with the hand-hold typically offers a slight rim, or lip, at the nether extremity, to prevent slippage.' My description of the baseball bat ran to 4500 words, all scratched with a diamond on the south wall. Does Shotwell read what I have written? I do not know. I am aware that Shotwell regards my writing-behavior as a little strange. Yet it is no stranger than his jacks-behavior, or the day he appeared in black bathing trunks with the .25 caliber Beretta strapped to his right calf and stood over the console, trying to span with his two arms outstretched the distance between the locks. He could not do it, I had already tried, standing over the console with my two arms outstretched, the distance is too great. I was moved to comment but did not comment, comment would have provoked countercomment, comment would have led God knows where. They had in their infinite patience, in their infinite foresight, in their infinite wisdom already imagined a man standing over the console with his two arms outstretched, trying to span with his two arms outstretched the distance between the locks.

Shotwell is not himself. He has made certain overtures. The burden of his message is not clear. It has something to do with the keys, with the locks. Shotwell is a strange person. He appears to be less affected by our situation than I. He goes about his business stolidly, watching the console, studying *Introduction to Marketing*, bouncing his rubber ball on the floor in a steady, rhythmical, conscientious manner. He appears to be less affected by our situation than I am. He is stolid. He says nothing. But he has made certain overtures, certain overtures have been made. I am not sure that I understand them. They have something to do with the keys, with the locks. Shotwell has something in mind. Stolidly he shucks the shiny silver paper from the frozen enchiladas, stolidly he stuffs them into the electric oven. But he has something in mind. But there must be a quid pro quo. I insist on a quid pro quo. I have something in mind.

I am not well. I do not know our target. They do not tell us for which city the bird is targeted. I do not know. That is planning. That is not my responsibility. My responsibility is to watch the console and when certain events take place upon the console, turn my key in the lock. Shotwell bounces the rubber ball on the floor in a steady, stolid, rhythmical manner. I am aching to get my hands on the ball, on the jacks. We have been here one hundred thirty-three days owing to an oversight. I write on the walls. Shotwell chants 'onesies, twosies, threesies, foursies' in a precise, well-modulated voice. Now he cups the jacks and the rubber ball in his hands and rattles them suggestively. I do not know for which city the bird is targeted. Shotwell is not himself.

Sometimes I cannot sleep. Sometimes Shotwell cannot sleep. Sometimes when Shotwell cradles me in his arms and rocks me to sleep, singing Brahms' 'Guten abend, gute Nacht,' or I cradle Shotwell in my arms and rock him to sleep, singing, I understand what it is Shotwell wishes me to do. At such moments we are very close. But only if he will give me the jacks. That is fair. There is something he wants me to do with my key, while he does something with his key. But only if he will give me my turn. That is fair. I am not well.

The Balloon

The balloon, beginning at a point on Fourteenth Street, the exact location of which I cannot reveal, expanded northward all one night, while people were sleeping, until it reached the Park. There, I stopped it; at dawn the northernmost edges lay over the Plaza; the free-hanging motion was frivolous and gentle. But experiencing a faint irritation at stopping, even to protect the trees, and seeing no reason the balloon should not be allowed to expand upward, over the parts of the city it was already covering, into the 'air space' to be found there, I asked the engineers to see to it. This expansion took place throughout the morning, soft imperceptible sighing of gas through the valves. The balloon then covered forty-five blocks north-south and an irregular area east-west, as many as six crosstown blocks on either side of the Avenue in some places. That was the situation, then.

But it is wrong to speak of 'situations,' implying sets

of circumstances leading to some resolution, some escape of tension; there were no situations, simply the balloon hanging there – muted heavy grays and browns for the most part, contrasting with walnut and soft yellows. A deliberate lack of finish, enhanced by skillful installation, gave the surface a rough, forgotten quality; sliding weights on the inside, carefully adjusted, anchored the great, vari-shaped mass at a number of points. Now we have had a flood of original ideas in all media, works of singular beauty as well as significant milestones in the history of inflation, but at that moment there was only *this balloon*, concrete particular, hanging there.

There were reactions. Some people found the balloon 'interesting.' As a response this seemed inadequate to the immensity of the balloon, the suddenness of its appearance over the city; on the other hand, in the absence of hysteria or other societally induced anxiety, it must be judged a calm, 'mature' one. There was a certain amount of initial argumentation about the 'meaning' of the balloon; this subsided, because we have learned not to insist on meanings, and they are rarely even looked for now, except in cases involving the simplest, safest phenomena. It was agreed that since the meaning of the balloon could never be known absolutely, extended discussion was pointless, or at least less purposeful than the activities of those who, for example, hung green and blue paper lanterns from the warm gray underside, in certain streets, or seized the occasion to write messages on the surface, announcing their availability for the performance of unnatural acts, or the availability of acquaintances.

Daring children jumped, especially at those points where the balloon hovered close to a building, so that the gap between balloon and building was a matter of a few inches, or points where the balloon actually made contact, exerting an ever-so-slight pressure against the side of a building, so that balloon and building seemed a unity. The upper surface was so structured that a 'landscape' was presented, small valleys as well as slight knolls, or mounds; once atop the balloon, a stroll was possible, or even a trip, from one place to another. There was pleasure in being able to run down an incline, then up the opposing slope, both gently graded, or in making a leap from one side to the other. Bouncing was possible, because of the pneumaticity of the surface, and even falling, if that was your wish. That all these varied motions, as well as others, were within one's possibilities, in experiencing the 'up' side of the balloon, was extremely exciting for children, accustomed to the city's flat, hard skin. But the purpose of the balloon was not to amuse children.

Too, the number of people, children and adults, who

took advantage of the opportunities described was not so large as it might have been: a certain timidity, lack of trust in the balloon, was seen. There was, furthermore, some hostility. Because we had hidden the pumps, which fed helium to the interior, and because the surface was so vast that the authorities could not determine the point of entry – that is, the point at which the gas was injected – a degree of frustration was evidenced by those city officers into whose province such manifestations normally fell. The apparent purposelessness of the balloon was vexing (as was the fact that it was 'there' at all). Had we painted, in great letters, 'LABORATORY TESTS PROVE' or '18% MORE EFFECTIVE' on the sides of the balloon, this difficulty would have been circumvented. But I could not bear to do so. On the whole, these officers were remarkably tolerant, considering the dimensions of the anomaly, this tolerance being the result of, first, secret tests conducted by night that convinced them that little or nothing could be done in the way of removing or destroying the balloon, and, secondly, a public warmth that arose (not uncolored by touches of the aforementioned hostility) toward the balloon, from ordinary citizens.

As a single balloon must stand for a lifetime of thinking about balloons, so each citizen expressed, in the attitude he chose, a complex of attitudes. One man might consider that the balloon had to do with the notion *sullied*, as in the sentence *The big balloon sullied the otherwise clear and radiant Manhattan sky*. That is, the balloon was, in this man's view, an imposture, something inferior to the sky that had formerly been there, something interposed between the people and their 'sky.' But in fact it was January, the sky was dark and ugly; it was not a sky you could look up into, lying on your back in the street, with pleasure, unless pleasure, for you, proceeded from having been threatened, from having been misused. And the underside of the balloon was a pleasure to look up into, we had seen to that, muted grays and browns for the most part, contrasted with walnut and soft, forgotten yellows. And so, while this man was thinking *sullied*, still there was an admixture of pleasurable cognition in his thinking, struggling with the original perception.

Another man, on the other hand, might view the balloon as if it were part of a system of unanticipated rewards, as when one's employer walks in and says, 'Here, Henry, take this package of money I have wrapped for you, because we have been doing so well in the business here, and I admire the way you bruise the tulips, without which bruising your department would not be a success, or at least not the success that it is.' For this man the balloon might be a brilliantly heroic 'muscle and pluck' experience, even if an experience poorly understood.

Another man might say, 'Without the example of —, it is doubtful that — would exist today in its present form,' and find many to agree with him, or to argue with him. Ideas of 'bloat' and 'float' were introduced, as well as concepts of dream and responsibility. Others engaged in remarkably detailed fantasies having to do with a wish either to lose themselves in the balloon, or to engorge it. The private character of these wishes, of their origins, deeply buried and unknown, was such that they were not much spoken of; yet there is evidence that they were widespread. It was also argued that what was important was what you felt when you stood under the balloon; some people claimed that they felt sheltered, warmed, as never before, while enemies of the balloon felt, or reported feeling, constrained, a 'heavy' feeling.

Critical opinion was divided:

'monstrous pourings'

         'harp'

XXXXXXX 'certain contrasts with darker portions'

   'inner joy'

'large, square corners'

'conservative eclecticism that has so far governed modern balloon design'

::::::: 'abnormal vigor'

'warm, soft lazy passages'

'Has unity been sacrificed for a sprawling quality?'

'Quelle catastrophe!'

'munching'

People began, in a curious way, to locate themselves in relation to aspects of the balloon: 'I'll be at that place where it dips down into Forty-seventh Street almost to the sidewalk, near the Alamo Chile House,' or, 'Why don't we go stand on top, and take the air, and maybe walk about a bit, where it forms a tight, curving line with the façade of the Gallery of Modern Art—' Marginal intersections offered entrances within a given time duration, as well as 'warm, soft, lazy passages' in which . . . But it is wrong to speak of 'marginal intersections,' each intersection was crucial, none could be ignored (as if, walking there, you might not find someone capable of turning your attention, in a flash, from old exercises to new exercises, risks and escalations). Each intersection was crucial, meeting of balloon and building, meeting of balloon and man, meeting of balloon and balloon.

It was suggested that what was admired about the balloon was finally this: that it was not limited, or defined. Sometimes a bulge, blister, or sub-section would carry all the way east to the river on its own initiative, in the manner of an army's movements on a map, as seen in a headquarters remote from the fighting. Then that part would be, as it were, thrown back again, or would withdraw into new dispositions; the next morning, that part would have made another sortie, or disappeared altogether. This ability of the balloon to shift its shape, to change, was very pleasing, especially to people whose lives were rather rigidly patterned, persons to whom change, although desired, was not available. The balloon, for the twenty-two days of its existence, offered the possibility, in its randomness, of mislocation of the self, in contradistinction to the grid of precise, rectangular pathways under our feet. The amount of specialized training currently needed, and the consequent desirability of long-term commitments, has been occasioned by the steadily growing importance of complex machinery, in virtually all kinds of operations; as this tendency increases, more and more people will turn, in bewildered inadequacy, to solutions for which the balloon may stand as a prototype, or 'rough draft.'

I met you under the balloon, on the occasion of your return from Norway; you asked if it was mine; I said it was. The balloon, I said, is a spontaneous autobiographical disclosure, having to do with the unease I felt at your absence, and with sexual deprivation, but now that your visit to Bergen has been terminated, it is no longer necessary or appropriate. Removal of the balloon was easy; trailer trucks carried away the depleted fabric, which is now stored in West Virginia, awaiting some other time of unhappiness, some time, perhaps, when we are angry with one another.

RYŪNOSUKE AKUTAGAWA *Hell Screen*

KINGSLEY AMIS *Dear Illusion*

SAUL BELLOW *Him With His Foot in His Mouth*

DONALD BARTHELME *Some of Us Had Been Threatening Our
Friend Colby*

SAMUEL BECKETT *The Expelled*

JORGE LUIS BORGES *The Widow Ching – Pirate*

PAUL BOWLES *The Delicate Prey*

ITALO CALVINO *The Queen's Necklace*

ALBERT CAMUS *The Adulterous Woman*

TRUMAN CAPOTE *Children on Their Birthdays*

ANGELA CARTER *Bluebeard*

RAYMOND CHANDLER *Killer in the Rain*

EILEEN CHANG *Red Rose, White Rose*

G. K. CHESTERTON *The Strange Crime of John Boulnois*

JOSEPH CONRAD *Youth*

ROBERT COOVER *Romance of the Thin Man and the
Fat Lady*

ISAK DINESEN *Babette's Feast*

MARGARET DRABBLE *The Gifts of War*

HANS FALLADA *Short Treatise on the Joys of Morphinism*

F. SCOTT FITZGERALD *Babylon Revisited*

IAN FLEMING *The Living Daylights*

E. M. FORSTER *The Machine Stops*

SHIRLEY JACKSON *The Tooth*

HENRY JAMES *The Beast in the Jungle*

M. R. JAMES *Canon Alberic's Scrap-Book*

JAMES JOYCE *Two Gallants*

FRANZ KAFKA *In the Penal Colony*

RUDYARD KIPLING *'They'*

D. H. LAWRENCE *Odour of Chrysanthemums*

PRIMO LEVI *The Magic Paint*

H. P. LOVECRAFT *The Colour Out Of Space*

MALCOLM LOWRY *Lunar Caustic*

CARSON MCCULLERS *Wunderkind*

KATHERINE MANSFIELD *Bliss*

ROBERT MUSIL *Flypaper*

VLADIMIR NABOKOV *Terra Incognita*

R. K. NARAYAN *A Breath of Lucifer*

FRANK O'CONNOR *The Cornet-Player Who Betrayed Ireland*

DOROTHY PARKER *The Sexes*

LUDMILLA PETRUSHEVSKAYA *Through the Wall*

JEAN RHYS *La Grosse Fifi*

SAKI *Filboid Studge, the Story of a Mouse That Helped*

ISAAC BASHEVIS SINGER *The Last Demon*

WILLIAM TREVOR *The Mark-2 Wife*

JOHN UPDIKE *Rich in Russia*

H. G. WELLS *The Door in the Wall*

EUDORA WELTY *Moon Lake*

P. G. WODEHOUSE *The Crime Wave at Blandings*

VIRGINIA WOOLF *The Lady in the Looking-Glass*

STEFAN ZWEIG *Chess*

a little history

Penguin Modern Classics were launched in 1961, and have been shaping the reading habits of generations ever since.

The list began with distinctive grey spines and evocative pictorial covers – a look that, after various incarnations, continues to influence their current design – and with books that are still considered landmark classics today.

Penguin Modern Classics have caused scandal and political change, inspired great films and broken down barriers, whether social, sexual or the boundaries of language itself. They remain the most provocative, groundbreaking, exciting and revolutionary works of the last 100 years (or so).

In 2011, on the fiftieth anniversary of the Modern Classics, we're publishing fifty Mini Modern Classics: the very best short fiction by writers ranging from Beckett to Conrad, Nabokov to Saki, Updike to Wodehouse. Though they don't take long to read, they'll stay with you long after you turn the final page.

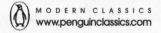

MODERN CLASSICS
www.penguinclassics.com